Quentin Blake

MRS ARMITAGE ON WHEELS

RED FOX

Mrs Armitage on Wheels

A Red Fox Book 978 0 099 40052 3

First published in Great Britain by Jonathan Cape Ltd 1987

Red Fox edition published 1999

an imprint of Random House Children's Publishers UK

21

Red Fox Books are published by Random House Children's Publishers UK

61-63 Uxbridge Road , LondonW5 5SA
A RANDOM HOUSE GROUP COMPANY
Addresses for companies within The Random House Group Limited
can be found at: www.randomhouse.co.uk/offices.htm

THE RANDOM HOUSE GROUP Limited Reg. No. 9554009

www.**randomhousechildrens**.co.uk

Printed and bound in China

Mrs Armitage was out on her bicycle.
Breakspear the dog ran alongside.

A hedgehog walked across the road.
Tring! Tring! went Mrs Armitage on the bell.

"What this bike needs," said Mrs Armitage to herself,
"is a really loud horn."

Mrs Armitage bought three horns.
They were all very loud.

Beep-beep

Honk-honk

Paheehahurh

went Mrs Armitage on her horns.

Then the chain came off.

By the time Mrs Armitage had got it on again her hands were all black and greasy.

"What this bike needs," said Mrs Armitage to herself,
"is somewhere to wash your hands."

So she got a bucket of water and a towel
and a soap-rack with a bar of soap,
and she hung them all on to the bike.
And off she went with
beautifully clean hands.

"What this bike needs," said Mrs Armitage to herself as she cycled along, "if it's to be looked after *properly*, is a complete tool kit."

So she got a toolbox
with spanners
and screwdrivers
and hammers and
cans of penetrating oil,
and she fixed it
on to the back of the bicycle,
and off she went.

By now Mrs Armitage was beginning to think about food. "What this bike needs," said Mrs Armitage to herself, "is somewhere to carry a light snack."

So she got a tray for apples and bananas and cheese-and-tomato sandwiches, and a holder for a bottle of lemonade and a flask of cocoa, and a special basket for bones and dog biscuits for Breakspear, and she fixed them all to the bike, and off they went.

But by now poor Breakspear was feeling quite tired, running along beside the bicycle. You could tell because his tongue was hanging out and he was panting. "What this bike needs," said Mrs Armitage to herself, "is something for a faithful dog to ride on."

So she got some iron brackets and some nuts and bolts
and some cushions, and she made a seat for
Breakspear, and off they went.

They had stopped beside the road for some
sandwiches and dog biscuits when it began to rain.
"Great heavens!" said Mrs Armitage. "What this
bike needs, Breakspear, is something to keep the
rain off."

So she got two umbrellas, one large, one small, and she fixed them up on the bicycle, and off they went.

Riding through the rain, Mrs Armitage began to feel
rather down-hearted. "What this bike needs," said
Mrs Armitage to herself, "is a bit of cheerful music.

So she got a transistor radio–cassette player and a lot of cassettes of cheerful music and a mouth-organ so that she could join in; and she fixed them all to the bike, and off they went.

Mrs Armitage was turning the pedals so fast and
blowing the mouth-organ so hard that soon she was
nearly exhausted.

"What this bike needs," said Mrs Armitage to
herself, "is a bit of extra oomph."

And so she got some wood and some ropes and some tarpaulin.

She rigged up a mast and a sail and she added a few yards of bunting and an anchor into the bargain.

And off they went with the wind behind them,
faster and faster and faster until ......

CRASH!

CRUNCH!

CLANG!

CLATTER!

THUD!

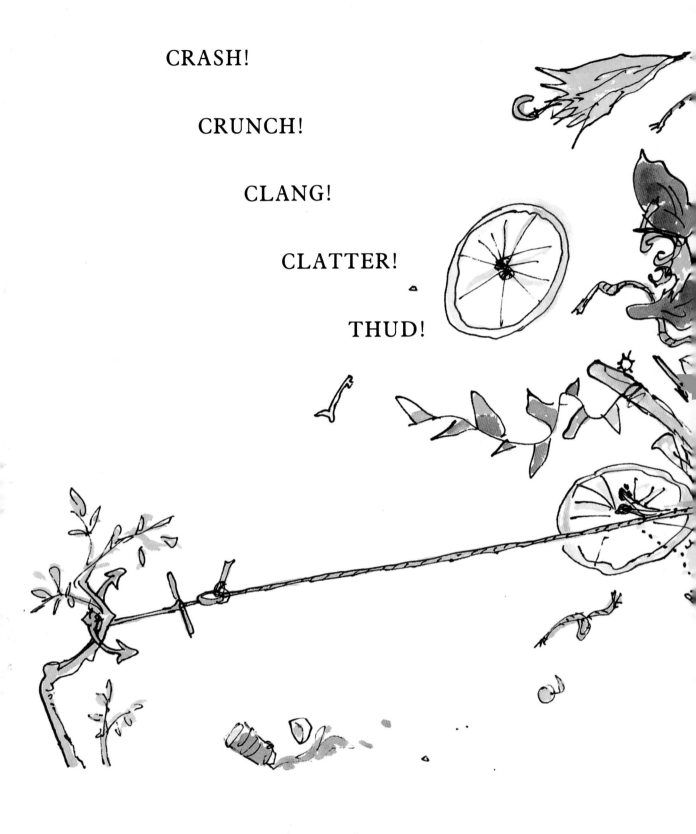

Paheehahurh!

"What this bike needs, Breakspear," said Mrs Armitage as she picked herself from the wreckage, "is taking to the dump."

"And what I need is......"

"Whoopeeeeeeeeeeeeee!"

"But what these roller-skates need," said Mrs
Armitage to herself, "what these roller-skates
need is . . . ."